Ghoulish Tales For The Brave

GITTE TAMAR

BTW LLC

To those who feel discomfort surrounding

the unknown, you are not alone; only if you

remain stuck in your anxiety should you be

allowed to mourn the death of your life

purpose, which you'll never come to know.

THANK YOU

Hello to all,

Thank you to every last one of you, no matter if your part was big or small.

Thank you to each of my family and friends, you already know who you are, so I will refrain from listing each of your specific names. Just know I will forever be thankful for each one of you who provided me with never-end-

ing troves of love and emotional support.

Thank you to all of my readers for continuing to embark on this journey with me. I am forever indebted to you.

Sincerely,

WARNING: Spooky content. Con-

tains references to gore, vio-

lence, kidnapping, and death.

TABLE OF CONTENTS

WITCHES SONG

By Gitte Tamar

Do you ever feel that some words only exist in your head?

Have you pondered why ghastly mortals scream, "You look dead!"

❦

Remember, they only see what lies skin deep, not the embedded secrets you quietly keep.

❦

So if they laugh at your novelty, welcome it with glee, for they only favor their own misery.

❦

Light a candle and close your eyes, does the flicker lure spells from the depths of your mind?

If the answer is yes, congratulations, our compositions align, and just like us, you possess the heart of a witch, and your in-

ner workings are of the magical
kind.

Now open your lids while you
face the flame, and we will do an-
other test to ensure the results
are the same.

Raise your hands in unison, does
your energy make the glimmer
grow?

Bravo to your success; you are
ready to go.

❡

We meet every full moon at mid-

night with broomsticks in hand

and recite our chants in a clear-

ing tucked away in the tim-

ber-filled land.

❡

The sky is the only place we

don't need to behave as we

dodge every treetop and each

fog-shrouded grave.

❡

We transcend into the clouds

and approach the moon,

recharging our souls while peer-

ing down at the smokestack
plumes.

Come with us; it is not half bad to
live a life with the magic others
only dream they had.

FAMOUS QUOTE FROM THE GRAVE

"INTERMISSION"

EDGAR A.
POE

(1809-1849)

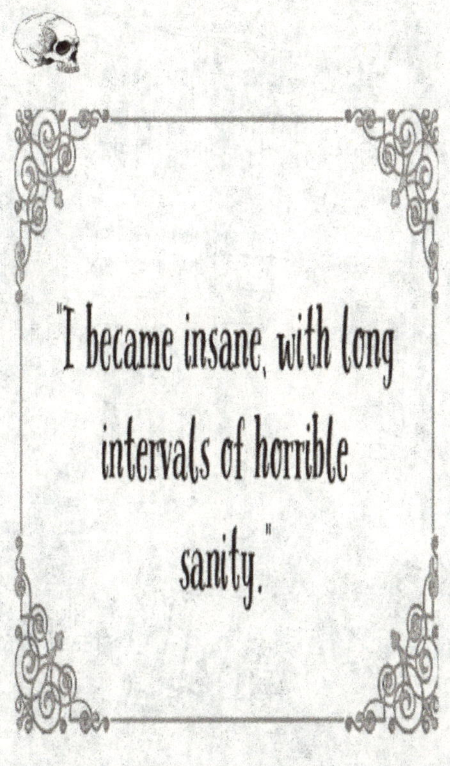

"I became insane, with long intervals of horrible sanity."

MY LAST TRICK OR TREAT

By Gitte Tamar

I loved to snack on anything sweet.

My favorite things were the chocolate pumpkins and gummy ghouls from the neighbor down the street.

My friends and I rapped on doors,

and when they opened wide, like

magic, a candy bowl appeared,

and happiness arrived.

Some people would give a single

piece and others a full-sized bar.

If lucky, you would score a goody

bag the size of a mason jar.

The night was all fun and games

until I reached the town's home

with the most haunted and omi-

nous tone.

I regret accepting the stupid bet of approaching the dwelling made of stone.

The signs were obvious that something wasn't right when I saw the yard overgrown and the window's black frosted panes that exuded no light.

I went forward anyway, even knowing the nightmarish lore.

The intelligent thing would have been to take a detour.

◊

I was proud to be the first person to walk to the door alone, but the mere sight of me standing at the entrance made my friends run in fear toward home.

◊

I knocked on the door, and the hinges released an eerie creak, and I thought, what luck, it is open, and I entered the home gleefully.

◊

The houses inside made me feel alright until I noticed hanging skins.

I touched the dried pieces to identify their origin, and they felt nothing like the cow leather to which I was akin.

The lesson I would like to share about roaming on Halloween night is always viewing each house with a bit of preemptive fright.

Heed my warning, or you may end up like me in a sinister home at the end of the street.

I assumed the man would offer me something to eat, but instead, he gave me eternal sleep.

FAMOUS QUOTE FROM THE GRAVE

"INTERMISSION"

WILLIAM

SHAKESPEARE

(1564-1616)

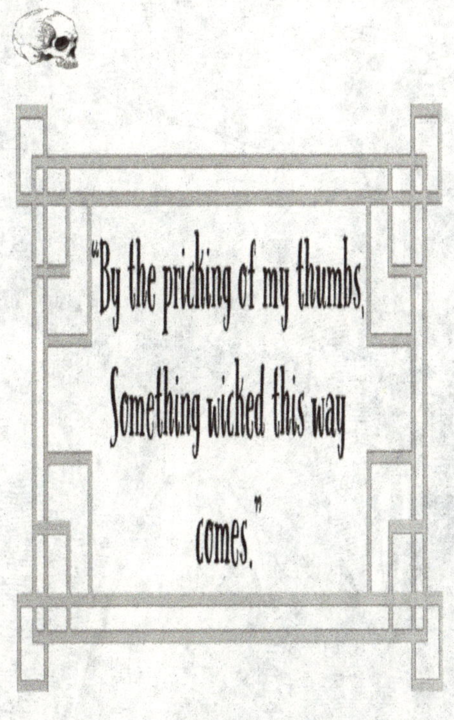

"By the pricking of my thumbs,

Something wicked this way

comes."

LAMENT OF A CRAZED POET

By Gitte Tamar

From childhood, poetry filled his head with beautiful melodies that many preferred to remain unsaid.

0

The more he read these lyrical
tales, the more the world's per-
secution was unveiled.

0

Each dawn, he peeped out his
window at the cloud's coverage
in the sky, and if melancholy in
appearance, he dreaded a storm
might arise.

0

He loathed being cold and damp,
and his mind would fret, over the
possibility of getting wet.

The longer he refused to step outside, the further his imagination came to life, and, in his chosen seclusion, creativity thrived.

Left in quiet solace without as much as a hello caused his paranoia over society's condemning scorn to grow.

He began worrying about the ominous narratives tormenting his dreams and his constant imagining of others' preemptive screams.

✣

He appeared not to care if the world hailed him as a lunatic, for he renounced a life of conformity based on the closed-minded views of hypocrites.

✣

Not wishing to endure ridicule or face subjection to harm, he hid away in his home, tending the stone fireplace that fueled his poetic charm.

✣

Word by word, he rejoiced in each tale he brought to life, and the more stories he penned, the less he tried to evade the dark-

ness he previously despised.

◊

For decades, he remained obliv-

ious over sealing his fate and his

work papers piled to the rafters

before realizing it was too late.

◊

Exhausted without any ideas left

in sight, his mind grew unbal-

anced from years of not seeing a

single lick of daylight.

◊

Huddled alone next to the fire,

his eyes turned dry, and for the

first time in his life, he found he could no longer cry.

๐

Having been reclusive for so long, he had forgotten his previous life, and each wrinkle revealed the years of being alone had been more bitter than nice.

๐

He recalled when he yearned for a family, specifically a wife, and even considered for a moment that a few pets might suffice.

๐

Carried away with the thoughts of what might have been, he

knew he must regain control by writing once again.

๏

He freed himself from strife, and from that day forward, with a clean slate, he commenced a new life.

๏

It was a radical decision that led to many sleepless nights, and on occasion he laid awake wondering if his drastic choice was right.

๏

His eyelids could not shake the exhaustion from his incessant writing leading up to that date, and with one last dip of his ink-

less quill, his mind drifted into a

trance-like state.

&

He would rest for the first time in

peace without a head filled with

nightmares of monstrous beasts.

&

As the neglected coals ignited

every paper to his left and right,

the flames cast a tremendous

glow on the slumbering man

who no longer had a will to fight.

&

Sadly, his story ends friendless,

with a quill in hand, surrounded

by the ashes of his life's work that he never had the pleasure in literary circles to defend.

No one ever came to appreciate the man's genius or learn his given name, but his haunting words can still be heard today, providing him a bit of fame.

So when you sit at your desk late at night and hear a frightful whisper tell you, "Go to bed," "it may just be the poet and not solely in your head.

If you find your creativity con-

fined, call like a crow three times,

and when you smell something

burning, he has arrived to help

you break your writer's block

and release the brilliance locked

inside your mind.

Just beware, it may be some-

thing you would rather not find.

FAMOUS QUOTE FROM THE GRAVE

"INTERMISSION"

BRAM
STOKER

(1847-1912)

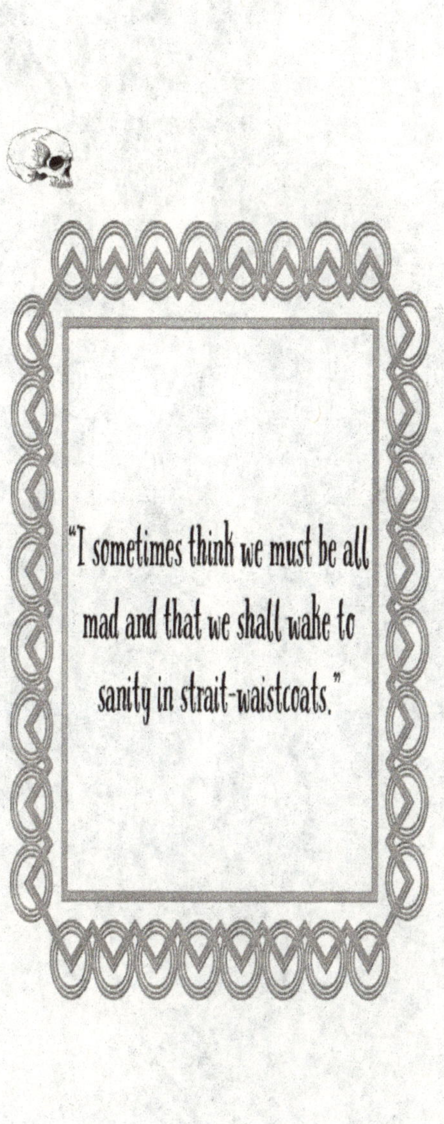

"I sometimes think we must be all
mad and that we shall wake to
sanity in strait-waistcoats."

WHAT IS FEAR?

By Gitte Tamar

Life would be dull without fear.

The amusement it creates is relatively clear, especially on Halloween, the scariest day of the year.

Children dressed as ghosts and goblins, glowing

jack-o'-lanterns, trick-or-treat-

ing, and legends recounted in

the dead of night make it simple

for an imaginative mind to take

flight.

&

There is excitement created by a

good scare or three.

Have you ever had a friend leap

out from behind a tree?

&

Did they shout "Boo"?

Did you then hide and surprise

them from a dark corner too?

Scaring the pants off someone can be fun; as an added bene-fit, you exercise when the fright makes you run.

Fantastic tales of monsters under the bed or graveyards filled with carnivorous dead can bring even the dullest of parties to laughter-filled tears and the memories made brings joy to our years.

What is life without fear?

Humdrum.

FAMOUS QUOTE FROM THE GRAVE

"INTERMISSION"

MARY
SHELLEY

(1797-1851)

"I looked upon the sea, it
was to be my grave"

JOIN US

By Gitte Tamar

Each night we wait with bated breath while your parents calm your dread, but as soon as you fall asleep, they step away from your bed.

Biting our tongues we peer at them with glee, as they overlook the glimmer of our porcelain pointy teeth.

*

They carefully check your clos-
et and underneath your bed, but
we find it silly when they don't
peek inside your head.

*

Their wiggling fingers through
the closing door and quiet good-
night, signal it is safe for our mis-
chief to take flight.

*

We travel into the darkest places
of your mind, we teach small
lessons that, during waking
hours, you often cannot find.

❦

Some of them serve as predic-
tions for a future date, and oth-
ers are simply tomfoolery cen-
tered on favorite games we like
to play.

❦

For those scared, do not fear.

It is something you will grow
used to since dreams occur year
after year.

❦

We use them to select whom
we invite to stay in our mon-
ster-filled castle somewhat far
away.

◊

If you pass our evaluation and

elect to follow us through the

golden gates, our tribe of misfits

will hail you as they greet us to

celebrate.

◊

Do not worry about the two gi-

ant creatures who left you to this

fate; they won't notice you're

missing until it's far too late.

◊

Upon their shocking revelation,

we will bite our tongues as we try

to hold our snickers over the fact

that we have won.

They will never get another chance to infiltrate our fun.

FAMOUS QUOTE FROM THE GRAVE

"INTERMISSION"

OSCAR WILDE

(1854-1900)

"They've promised that dreams can come true- but forgot to mention that nightmares are dreams, too."

WE ARE MONSTERS

By Gitte Tamar

We are monsters, small and fluffy, and some of us are tall and scruffy.

If your bedroom is where we choose to stay, we call dibs on the closet, as it's our favored place to play.

◊

We will tell you hello on moonlit

midnights when darkness allows

us to linger out of sight.

◊

During daylight hours, you may

hear us growl or moan, which

is another way to recognize that

you are not alone.

◊

Our shuffling creaks may cause

you to shriek, but have no fear,

for we are meek and unable to

run because of the clumsy nature

of our unusually tiny feet.

It doesn't matter whom you tell,

for we know your parents very

well.

As children, they too fell under

our mysterious spell, and in their

closets, we would dwell.

Once settled, we will never roam

because we cherish the bed-

rooms we call home.

FAMOUS QUOTE FROM THE GRAVE

"INTERMISSION"

ROBERT LOUIS STEVENSON

(1850-1894)

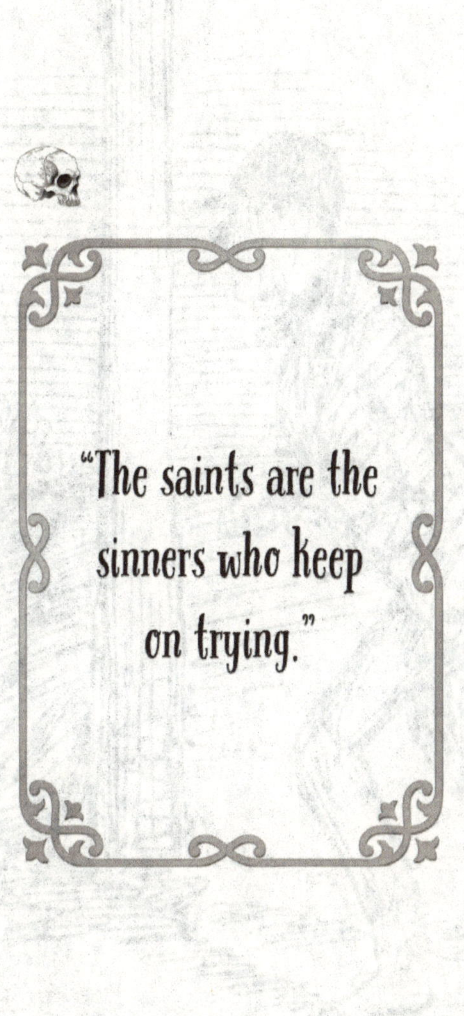

"The saints are the
sinners who keep
on trying."

HAVE YOU SEEN MY RED BALL?

By Gitte Tamar

My favorite red ball vanished a few days ago.

I knew I had lost it somewhere

deep in the snow.

❦

One stormy night, I took a blanket and hunted for the toy unchaperoned.

Wandering through the darkness, I lost view of my cozy home.

❦

Not a single soul answered my tearful cry as I hollered for help through the starless sky.

❦

I pushed onward, shivering and alone, convinced I would find the red rubber sphere I once joyfully owned.

For a moment, I believed I spotted the orb in plain sight, but it was just an illusion, and disappointed, I continued trudging through the blizzard-filled night.

Like the ball, I found myself lost in the icy cold, and, giving up, I lay down with my blanket as the snowstorm's wintry character took hold.

My body and limbs tingled, then solidly froze, and one eye remained stuck open, staring at

the little red ball tauntingly

perched right in front of my nose.

FAMOUS QUOTE FROM THE GRAVE

"INTERMISSION"

EDGAR A. POE

(1809-1849)

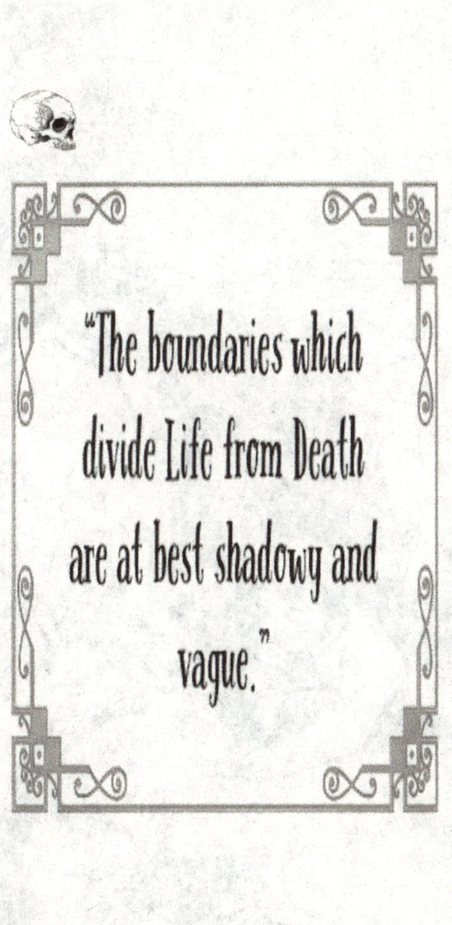

"The boundaries which divide Life from Death are at best shadowy and vague."

REST
IN
PEACE

GOULISH FLIGHT

By Gitte Tamar

After assuring no single soul is in sight, I take off from the ground and fly to the highest heights.

It's the winter's most treacher-ous night, but the waterlogged wind does not hinder my flight.

9

I soar like a kite around the raised stone that everyone believes is now my home.

9

Gliding past the fresh pile of mud and clay, I scan the chiseled names marking row after row of mounded graves, where I assume more corpses silently play.

9

Nothing can stop my ghoulish glee as I float in the air peacefully.

FAMOUS QUOTE FROM THE GRAVE

"INTERMISSION"

OSCAR WILDE

(1854-1900)

"Behind every exquisite
thing that existed,
there was something
tragic."

VAMPIRE'S REVENGE

By Gitte Tamar

Do you find yourself lonesome like me?

Have you ever been trapped inside a musty coffin, wishing to be free?

Occasionally I wish I could step outside in the daylight hours, but the sun is quite unfriendly, and though I would prefer to try, I

know the glare would cause me

to fry and inconveniently die.

Though most already consider

me dead, I think becoming a pile

of ashes would further my dread.

There must be some reason why

I was condemned to this strife.

Perhaps it's a karmic lesson from

my acts in a previous life.

Can it be that someone would in-

tentionally choose this fate?

This existence is not for me, for residing in a wooden box is a deplorable eternal state.

Woe is me, my poor soul; I lost myself many lifetimes ago.

Falling in love did me in by subjecting me to a life of voracious sin.

They deemed her the most beautiful of all dames.

Maria was her name.

❧

I found myself lured into a tumultuous ride from the moment I saw her golden hair and piercing ice-blue eyes, and with her first hello, I became mesmerized by each of her treacherous lies.

❧

I was oblivious to my impending fate until our wedding night when Maria mutated into a horrific beast exposing her grisly plight.

The monsters from Van Helsing's tales could not match the terrifying sight.

Her teeth transformed into jagged fangs with bloody stains, and her eyes turned to the blackest black, confirming her soulless remains.

Her delicate porcelain skin withered to confirm her exact age, and her once luxurious hair tumbled to the ground as she carried on in a fit of rage.

Though her beauty was gone and raised the alarm, her siren song captivated me, and I felt more

entranced by her deviant charm.

I recall very little from the night

she drained every bit of juice in

my veins and flew off with her

blood thirst that never wanes.

Upon arising the following day

to rays of sunshine peeking

through the window bay, my

aversion to their brightness filled

me with dismay.

Confronting my fear, I stared in

the beveled glass mirror, hoping

to view my expression, but dis-
covered no reflection.

How can this be that I find myself
tricked into a life of butchery?

I have heard tales of victims
plagued by this tragic fate, and
it appears, like the others, that I
discovered the truth far too late.

Each night when I feast alone in
my chamber, I dream of the day I
take vengeance on the cruel per-
petrator.

I will see to her final breath and

conniving hearts' last beat, for

only with her extermination will I

rest in a peaceful sleep.

FAMOUS QUOTE FROM THE GRAVE

"INTERMISSION"

BRAM STOKER

(1847-1912)

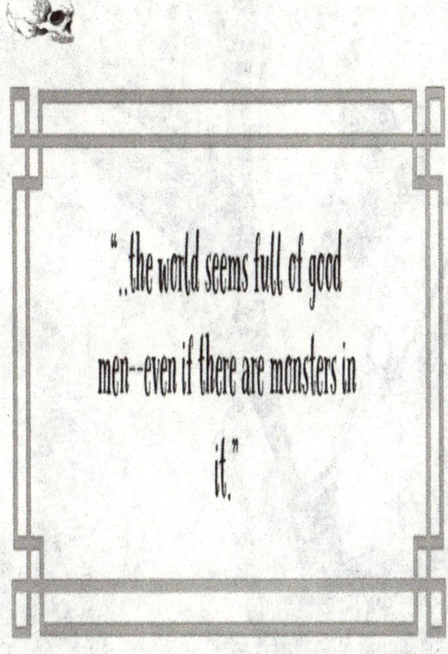
"..the world seems full of good

men--even if there are monsters in

it."

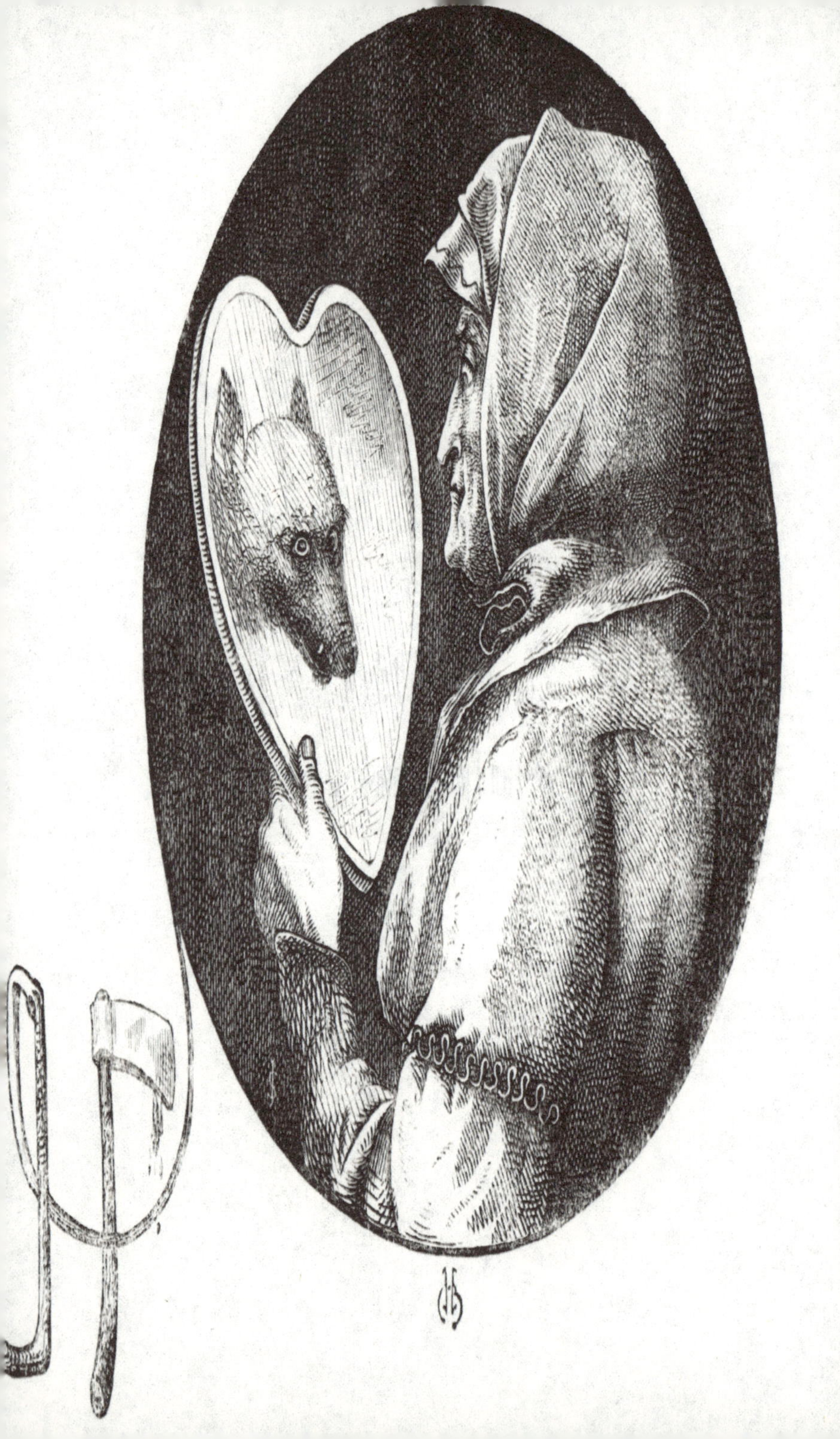

HOWL

By Gitte Tamar

Darkness swept the tree-tops, warning all the in-sects to crowd back into their moss-covered knots.

I chose to only walk through the forest during the day because, like the bugs, something about the night pushed me away.

◊

I worked all day until the sun

fell over my head and slumbered

when it was dark, safe in my bed.

◊

Each night as I hid beneath my

sheets, the wind filled my ears

with whines and creaks.

Curiously, I found them pleasant

when they sounded like enticing

shrieks.

◊

I wondered why I felt content-

ment in every horrible moan.

Had I lost my mind or, worse yet, my soul?

Or, maybe perhaps I was just comfortable being alone.

❦

When I was young, I heard stories of midnight creatures walking the land.

Everyone would tell me how they would howl at the moon to gather their clan.

❦

Desperate to get the lurking thoughts out of my head, I lived out my imagination when tucked in my bed.

◊

I dreamt of growing four strong paws, fur, and pointed teeth and felt my transformed body traveling through the woods effortlessly.

◊

The more the idea would steep, the greater my dreams would creep into the dens where I imagined they would sleep.

◊

The more my true identity took hold, the more I found solace in the dark closet of my log-sculpted country abode.

❡

Wanting a family, I tried till the end to reunite with the beasts I was sure were my long-lost kin.

❡

Oddly they never answered my calls as I howled from my improvised cave, but I made a vow that I would keep trying until my dying day.

That time came quicker than I imagined, and the closet became my grave.

❡

Sadly, no one knew my life had come to an end since decades

had passed without a single vis-

iting friend.

I hope the kindred creatures hear

my corpses cry when the next full

moon shines bright in the sky.

Only then will my spirit be al-

lowed to fly from my makeshift

den hidden away in the wooded

glen.

FAMOUS QUOTE FROM THE GRAVE

"INTERMISSION"

ROBERT

LOUIS

STEVENSON

(1850-1894)

"Dead men don't bite."

DREARY SKY

By Gitte Tamar

The clouds became irritated with the prospect of another sunny day, so they caught an airy current and joyously drifted away.

"Who will help me escape?" The wind cried. "This isn't fair. Why am I stuck here swirling around the sky? No one but me under-

stands the dread of being held

captive up this high?"

❦

Craving to experience everything

mortal, especially the ability to

talk, desperate, the wind even

briefly considered becoming a

dog as long as it barked and

walked.

❦

It attempted to control its anger

by whistling a merry tune, but

the growing resentment over

other people's freedoms turned

the dancing breeze into an omi-

nous gale of doom.

The gusty air plagued the val-
ley with unrelenting hail to prove
its worth and punish those who
walked the earth.

All the people peered out their
windows and released a unified
cry that they were tired of the
weather and hoped the storm
would subside.

"No, more!" They shouted at the
sky. "No, more! We implore you;
you are ruining our lives. Please,

make it go away so we can go outside."

§

The wind listened with unsympathetic ease while pretending to sip tea steeped in their pitiful pleas and basking in its happiness over the plan's brilliant treachery.

With a roar of thunder, its cackle boomed over the mountains and through trees.

§

"Alas!", The wind said with a devious grin. "Someone is finally miserable like me."

FAMOUS QUOTE FROM THE GRAVE

"INTERMISSION"

EDGAR A. POE

(1809-1849)

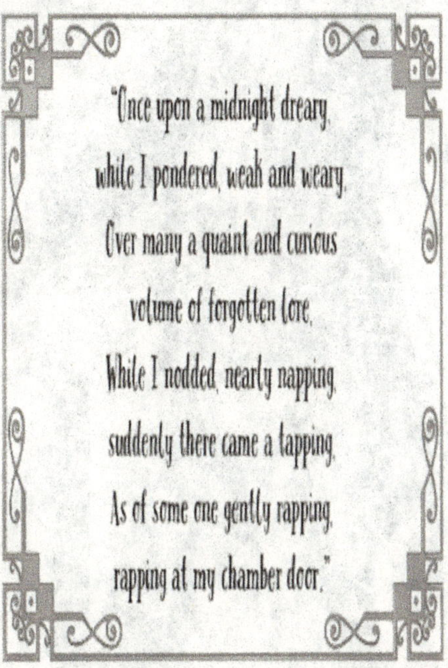

"Once upon a midnight dreary,
while I pondered, weak and weary,
Over many a quaint and curious
volume of forgotten lore,
While I nodded, nearly napping,
suddenly there came a tapping,
As of some one gently rapping,
rapping at my chamber door."

THE HEADLESS MAN

By Gitte Tamar

I was strolling home alone one night, and, to my dismay, a hand reached out from the darkness and snatched my top hat away.

One moment it was peacefully

sitting upon my skull, and the

next, without warning, ripped

from my body, head and all.

The hostility of the encounter

was utterly unprovoked; I never

so much as stirred a single con-

flict or performed a cruel joke.

I am certain they must be aware

by now that on the top hat, a

curse resides.

The item brings with it great for-tune but at the whim of a devilish side.

Like the plethora of holders be-fore me, the hat's intentions will be unveiled through their luck's swift change of tides.

§

I hope whoever pinched the lid from my head holds a deep ap-preciation for the item's finely woven cashmere threads.

§

They had best enjoy the thing swiftly before another greedy soul snatches it maliciously.

❡

Now, like a specter, I roam the

pavements to hunt for my prized

possession.

There is no change to my dai-

ly routine as I scour the earth in

search of the thief fueling my ob-

session.

❡

As I track the fiend who, in the

dark of night, left me for dead

and without a chance to fight, I

shout to them this phrase with

all of my might, "My hat, my hat,

the one that sat upon my head,

give it to me, now, or you will

wish you were dead. Your life will

face horrors far worse than mine

if you don't return, my dear top

hat. I will only ask one time," I still

find it hard to believe my pre-

cious hat was taken from me.

The culprit left no trace of their

thievery, aside from my horrify-

ing harm.

I will forever be haunted by the

fateful night when I plunged to

the alley's floor, and without as

much a clue, my life would be no

more.

◊

Cruelly, the hat's curse contin-

ues to deny me rest, even af-

ter I have taken my last breath

and my heart's rhythm no longer

beats in my chest.

◊

So, I will inquire once more, have

you come across my hat?

◊

My beloved accouterment that

a short time ago was happily

perched on top of my head?

I implore you to return the thing

to my freshly shoveled bed.

❦

Until its arrival, I will lay awake deep in the ground, underneath this worm-infested mound, awaiting the day when my precious hat is found.

❦

With bated breath, I linger in anticipation of the momentous day when I can escape this purgatory and free myself from this bodies rotting decay.

FAMOUS QUOTE FROM THE GRAVE

"INTERMISSION"

WILLIAM

SHAKESPEARE

(1564-1616)

FIRST WITCH
Round about the cauldron go;
In the poison'd entrails throw.
Toad, that under cold stone
Days and nights has thirty-one
Swelter'd venom sleeping got,
Boil thou first i' the charmed pot.
ALL
Double, double toil and trouble;
Fire burn, and cauldron bubble.
SECOND WITCH
Fillet of a fenny snake,
In the cauldron boil and bake;
Eye of newt and toe of frog,
Wool of bat and tongue of dog,
Adder's fork and blind-worm's sting,
Lizard's leg and owlet's wing,
For a charm of powerful trouble,
Like a hell-broth boil and bubble.
ALL
Double, double toil and trouble;
Fire burn and cauldron bubble.
THIRD WITCH
Scale of dragon, tooth of wolf,
Witches' mummy, maw and gulf
Of the ravin'd salt-sea shark,
Root of hemlock digg'd i' the dark,
Liver of blaspheming Jew,
Gall of goat, and slips of yew
Silver'd in the moon's eclipse,
Nose of Turk and Tartar's lips,
Finger of birth-strangled babe
Ditch-deliver'd by a drab,
Make the gruel thick and slab;
Add thereto a tiger's chaudron,
For the ingredients of our cauldron.
ALL
Double, double toil and trouble;
Fire burn and cauldron bubble (4.1.4-36).

ABOUT AUTHOR

Gitte Tamar

Brigitte, "Gitte," Tamar was born in a small rural Oregon town. Growing up, she was enthralled by scary tales featuring poetic tones and consistently gravitated towards writing darkened narratives. In the different storylines, Brigitte explores the harsh realities of social issues faced by today's generations. This includes the dark outcomes brought on by peer pressure, addiction, homelessness, mental illness, childhood trauma, and abuse. She feels it is essential to share narratives that refrain from sugarcoating the topics society tends to shy away from.